Self-Esteem

A Teen's Guide to Finding Personal
Success with a Proven Program of
Cognitive Techniques

Samantha Koffler

Table of Contents

Additionally, the information in the following pages is intended only for informational purposes and should thus be thought of as universal. As befitting its nature, it is presented without assurance regarding its prolonged validity or interim quality. Trademarks that are mentioned are done without written consent and can in no way be considered an endorsement from the trademark holder.

Introduction

People who have no self-esteem often think that they will become confident and happy with themselves when their current situation changes. Seeing a beautiful face when you look into the mirror will make you walk with your shoulders high up; having caring parents will make you feel normal and happy, scoring all A's in your exam will enable you to look at your classmates in the eye and say whatever you want, your neighbors will respect you when you own a car and that will boost your confidence, getting married will elevate your status and in turn, make you feel less inferior about yourself.

Self-esteem or the lack thereof is related to external circumstances. "If A or B happens, my self-esteem will increase," so they think. While it is possible that you will see yourself in a better light and get a sense of self-worth from achieving great things, that level of highness you feel will most likely not last. Why? Self-esteem is basically a state of mind. Although the current state of your life and other people's opinion of you may have a bearing on your self-esteem, the ultimate determinant of your self-esteem is your thoughts.

Take this scenario for instance: Unemployed Miss A thinks Miss B who is employed is more intelligent and better than she is. Employed Miss B tells herself that she would have been running her own business by now if only she was as smart and efficient as her entrepreneur friend. Then, there is Miss C who is also unemployed but thinks her situation is not because of her not being good enough but because she is yet to develop the skills needed for the job.

What differentiates Miss C from both Miss A and Miss B? The way she sees herself. Miss C understands that she doesn't possess the skills that will land her the job she wants but instead of thinking there is something inherently wrong with her, she singles out the problem and separates it from her core being. Between Miss C and Miss B, who do you think lives a happy life? It's Miss C of course. As humans, we are aware of our identity: hating the way we look, how we act or the family we come from automatically cripples our sense of self-worth. Your level of self-esteem usually depends on how much you like and appreciate yourself.

Don't confuse healthy self-esteem with too high or 'overly inflated' self-esteem though. Thinking you are superior to everybody is just as psychologically unhealthy as seeing yourself as the dust of the earth— the worst being on earth, undeserving of love. You overestimate your abilities, praise yourself too much and expect others to do the same even when you don't deserve it. Other people are seen through a diminishing lens and you act as though the world revolves around you.

Having self-esteem that is too high is dangerous and damaging, especially because it prevents you from embracing self-improvement.

The segment of this examines the dimensions of self-esteem further, your aim should be to have a moderate self-esteem.

Chapter 1: What Healthy Self-Esteem Means

There are many definitions of self-esteem. Healthy self-esteem is about consistently valuing who you are, feeling positive about your identity, having realistic expectations of yourself, and acting in ways that demonstrate self-respect and adherence to your own values.

In other words, building self-esteem is about learning to believe in your own worth and accept who you are: a human with both strengths and weaknesses, just like everyone else. By understanding that, you can begin to explore new ideas, learn new skills, and practice tools to move beyond insecurities and feel more confident.

Natalie's Story

Natalie's mom first brought her to see me when she was in middle school, saying they were really struggling at home. Natalie refused to ride the school bus in the morning, resulting in fights with her parents, who ultimately ended up having to drive her to school. Her mom said the issue was making her and her husband late for work and was causing a lot of friction in the family.

When I first met Natalie, she sat with her arms folded across her chest and responded to all my questions with one-word answers and shoulder shrugs. It was clear she wasn't happy to be there. But after I explained that this was a safe space to discuss anything she wanted; Natalie softened a bit. She began telling me how awkward she felt at the bus stop where she waited with a group of popular girls who were in the grade above her. Natalie felt like a loser standing there alone while they laughed and gossiped about their peers, barely noticing her.

I empathized with what she was experiencing. Middle school and high school can be rough socially! It's sometimes hard to find your place among the cliques and various groups of established friends.

Over the next few months, Natalie and I worked on ways she could cope with the fear of being judged and armed her with skills to feel more comfortable at the bus stop. She didn't become close friends with that particular group of girls, but she got to the point where she could exchange friendly smiles with them each morning and in the hallways, which helped her feel less isolated and more comfortable being herself. People with healthy self-esteem view themselves as worthwhile and good enough. They can recognize their positive qualities while also accepting that they are imperfect and will inevitably have flaws and face challenges and setbacks. They don't keep beating themselves up about their limitations. Instead, they just put things in perspective so that their imperfections don't drag them down.

People with healthy self-esteem can trust in their own judgment. They can express their own beliefs, wants, and needs without getting caught up with fear. They find healthy ways to deal with the chaos of peer pressure and avoid getting trapped in harmful patterns and destructive behaviors. They can recognize when relationships are unhealthy and dysfunctional, and they take steps to protect themselves by distancing themselves from toxic people.

People who can achieve a healthy level of self-esteem maintain realistic expectations of themselves and others. They feel deserving of respect, and they extend the same level of respect to others. They recognize that self-esteem comes from within, from a fundamental belief that you are okay, and that it can't be earned externally by seeking the approval or validation of others.

If like most teens, your self-esteem is not in an optimal place, the idea of healthy self-esteem may seem like a lofty pipe dream. But I promise you, the awareness and new skills you will learn in this book—if you put them into practice—will land you on the path to becoming the happy, confident, self-assured person you want to be.

Chapter 2: What You Stand to Gain from Healthy Self-Esteem

Improving your self-esteem has many benefits, like being able to trust in yourself and follow your own instincts. You can take pride in your accomplishments and feel a sense of purpose and hope for the future. You learn to feel comfortable in your own skin and make decisions without always relying on everyone else to decide for you. You become more self-assured and less likely to procrastinate or second-guess your opinions and choices. For example, if your friends ask you what movie you want to see, you can give your honest opinion without fear that it won't be what they want to see. When self-esteem is healthy, you worry less about what everyone else thinks and rise above feelings of self-doubt and fear.

As self-esteem improves, you can avoid getting caught up in a cycle of self-blame and negative thinking. You can accept your mistakes, knowing that they are inevitable in life and provide valuable lessons and opportunities for growth. You can recognize that the effort you put in is just as important, if not more so than the result. If you get a C on a test, for example, instead of beating yourself up for not getting an A, you recognize that either you did the best you could or maybe didn't study hard enough. You can then decide to get extra help or study more in the future. When your self-esteem is intact, you can view one bad grade or failed class as a disappointment but not the end of the world.

It also means you're able to find a stable balance of independence and interdependence. You can enjoy spending time alone but also form relationships that are healthy and secure rather than clingy or overbearing. You come to expect honesty and equality in relationships as you establish healthy boundaries, which sets you up to have better experiences when it comes to dating and friendships. People with high self-esteem are less likely to be manipulated or treated poorly by others, and they know when to walk away from an unhealthy situation. They also communicate well with others and are assertive in situations where they need to speak up, including asking for help without feelings of shame or embarrassment.

Positive self-esteem enables you to interact in healthy ways with others and avoid engaging in behaviors like bullying, teasing, or putting others down in a misguided attempt to feel powerful or liked. Instead, you know and follow your own values, and you can make your own choices without succumbing to peer pressure or becoming paralyzed by fear of being judged. You can navigate the new experiences and temptations that high school brings with confidence rather than anxiety about fitting in. Friendships are fulfilling and fun rather than overwhelming and filled with drama and chaos. You're able to say "no" and stand your ground without feeling like a loser or fearing rejection.

Another great thing about positive self-esteem is that you can better balance everything you have on your plate because you will develop the skills to better manage the stress and pressures that are so prevalent in high school. Basically, improving self-esteem can help you like yourself more and go through life more comfortably and with a greater sense of security in who you are.

Chapter 3: Common Signs of Low Self-Esteem

To help us from falling into the trap of having low self-esteem, it is important to know what the symptoms or the warning signs are. Then we can address whatever the cause is and work on bettering that aspect of ourselves and turning it into a positive. We exude our state of emotional wellbeing to the outside world. Thus, how we feel and what we think about can be seen by those who cross our path. We attract what we put out into the world – this is known as the "law of attraction".

So, when our self-esteem is low, we will attract more of the same in our lives.

But when we have a healthy level of self-esteem, we will attract more positivity, joy, happiness, and a sense of wellbeing and abundance into our lives. We will find that life will have more appeal to us than when our self-esteem is low.

When we are happy and have a healthy level of self-esteem, we have the desire to do things and a desire to achieve and better our lives. You then have a sense of zest for life, which may also urge you to live a very sociable life.

We do experience days where we feel a little "down" but this is where it is important to know what the signs and symptoms are of low self-esteem, so you can take action if action is needed.

Some of the most common signs of low self-esteem that one should look out for, are the following:

- Lack of confidence.
- Fearful behavior.
- Inability to be assertive.
- Pretentiousness.
- Anti-social behavior.
- Indecisiveness.
- Rebelliousness.
- Lack of generosity or empathy.
- Materialism.

Lack of Confidence

When we have low self-esteem, this results in a lack of self-confidence. People who have low self-confidence have little or no faith in themselves and/or their abilities. They normally seek the approval of others. Although they may not really need their approval, these individuals have a dire need to feel appreciated.

Generally, people who have low self-confidence do not have an extremely high opinion of themselves and may experience a feeling that they somehow "fall short" in comparison to others. Some also tend to appear shy or introverted.

Another sign of low self-confidence is boastfulness. Some people boast about their existent and/or non-existent achievements. They have a need to feel superior to others, but they know that they are not over-achievers and they are in fact not really achieving anything better than anyone else.

Fearful Behavior

Generally, these individuals are fearful of everything in life. They will try to hide from anybody, be invisible, blend into a crowd and, make themselves insignificant.

Such individuals generally have a fear of change and a fear of trying new things in life. They do not particularly enjoy facing new situations in their lives. They prefer not to draw any attention to themselves. Some people also have a fear of attending functions where they are faced with the possibility of meeting new people and their uncertainty of how they will fit in.

This could also include a fear of traveling alone and a fear of taking risks in life. For some, this even includes the fear of leaving their home. (Which serves as a "safety blanket" for them).

They generally prefer things to stay as they are. These individuals are also prone to pleasing and/or obeying everyone except themselves.

Inability to be Assertive

These individuals generally find it exceedingly difficult to say "no" to anybody or even stand up for their own rights. They are unable to assert themselves.

People who lack assertiveness find it difficult to express their opinions, feelings, and their beliefs towards others in an open and honest manner. Individuals who lack assertiveness generally have an inability to put their own ideas and thoughts forward. They are also often not straight forward and tend to sell themselves short. They may also come across to others as being submissive.

These individuals are generally non-confrontational, as they feel unable to defend themselves and to stand up for what they believe. They may land up in situations where they are under too much pressure but are unable to say so.

On a negative note, they can often be aggressive. But this aggression is indicative of "false inner strength." These individuals are not aggressive, as aggressive behavior is more indicative of self-enhancing behavior.

Being assertive means having the ability to "speak your mind" (in a gentle manner) and to say "no" when you really feel the need to...

Pretentiousness

These individuals pretend to be someone or something which they are not, purely for the purpose of keeping up appearances. They spend money that they cannot really afford to and tend to buy things that they do not really need.

They will generally try to impress everyone in any possible way they can. These individuals have a dire need to be admired and respected by others. They also have a need to fit in and be accepted.

At a social gathering, these individuals could be labeled as the "light of the party." They generally enjoy the attention and tend to overspend when entertaining friends and family.

They tend to overcompensate with material possessions, but also in the way they come across to others. It is not about making other people feel bad about themselves. It is more about their need to feel good about themselves.

Anti-Social Behavior

These individuals are often also attention seekers. As they are generally ignored by people and will resort to doing things that will gain the attention of others. Sometimes these individuals will also commit acts which attract negative attention. But they perceive negative attention as still being attention. To them, some form of attention is better than no attention at all.

Anti-social behavior is generally considered as either disobedient or angry (aggressive) behavior or it may also be considered as rebellious or uncooperative behavior.

People who show signs of anti-social behavior generally tend to be withdrawn. They can resort to either aggressive or uncooperative behavior. But this depends on the individual and various other factors. Most of the time people tend to show signs of anti-social behavior when they are in their teens.

However, in such a case where this is not just a "teenage phase," these teenagers can grow up having personality disorders later in their lives.

A good example of anti-social behavior would be the "very popular naughty child."

Indecisiveness

These individuals find it difficult to decide. There are various factors which may hinder their ability to make a firm decision.

They have a fear of being criticized, judged, and even a lack of courage prohibits these individuals from making decisions. Thus, absolving them from any form of responsibility.

They can be indecisive about anything, from doing something exceedingly small, choosing something from a menu, or taking a new job. On a bigger scale, they could be indecisive about making serious life-changing decisions.

Fear is one of the big driving forces behind indecisiveness and can prevent these individuals from finding happiness, from finding the right life partner and from changing their lives.

This hinders self-growth, self-confidence, and to an extent one's level of independence and individuality. Thus, this can also affect various areas of one's life. Not deciding, is like choosing to do nothing at all...

Rebellious Behavior

These individuals will rebel either in a positive or a negative way. This is another form of seeking attention and/or getting their point across.

Once again, also to these individuals any form of attention is still attention. Whether this is in a negative or a positive form.

One good example of such behavior is when someone has been told or urged not to do something and yet the person will turn around and do exactly that, out of a sense of "spite" to others.

There are individuals though, who will act rebelliously, just for the sake of rebelling, even though they may know that they are wrong in some way.

This can rather be a cry for attention or help, rather than an act performed out of sheer spite to another. Sometimes these individuals do not even realize what signals their behavior is sending out to others.

Lack of Generosity and Empathy

These individuals lack a sense of generosity and empathy. They perceive themselves as being undeserving. They are not really "givers."

They cannot give, because for them they cannot receive, as they feel unworthy of receiving. They find it difficult to compliment others or even receive compliments themselves.

Generally, when these people receive a compliment, they will not thank the person for it, but rather comment about how old something is or respond with a question, such as "are you really sure?"

This is not out of disrespect or ungratefulness, but rather their own sense of unworthiness. They do not feel that they are deserving of any compliments. This is nearly a foreign concept to some.

For them, it is even difficult to help others and to support charities and/or donate money towards a worthy cause. They tend to hold on to what they have and do not get rid of just anything.

Materialism

These individuals attach a lot of value to material possessions and wealth. They generally judge others not by their qualities, but by their material possessions.

One will find that exists a lot of competition in the lives of people who are materialistic. There is always one person competing with another and there is a dire need to own the best of everything.

They would generally try to be "one-up" on the next person and these individuals are not necessarily shy about showcasing their material possessions.

They generally tend to look down on those who are less fortunate and to them, the only people who really count are people of the same monetary and/or social standing as themselves.

They tend to perceive rich people to be more valuable (and important) than poor people; irrespective of the qualities which these people may possess.

Chapter 4: Boosting your Self-Confidence in Steps

Low self-confidence is something that stems from within oneself. The more terrible you feel about what your identity is and what you do, the less motivation you will have to take the necessary steps to construct your self-confidence. From that point, it is easy to fall into a cycle of negative and irrational reasoning, keeping you buried in harmful and inaccurate ideas about yourself. How can you stop this endless loop and start moving in a progressive, positive way? It's a process, and it won't occur without any preparation, but there are things that you can change and keep it moving.

Having sound confidence is extremely significant as it ultimately leads to you making constructive decisions in your daily life and gives you the mental strength to be yourself and to have positive connections. All these benefits would help you manage troublesome circumstances. It's critical to accept the fact that you can change and that, in general, all humans are capable of change. Change does not happen overnight, but it happens consistently throughout our lives.

Though it does not seem doable, if you have a low level of self-confidence, there are various things you can do to raise it to a higher level. It is not inherited, and an individual is not required to depend on anyone but themselves to build up their level of self-confidence. Also, the moment you realize that no situation is permanent and that you will not be able to control everything, then you can start working on your confidence. At that moment, you could start working on yourself and accepting that you deserve respect despite what others say about you.

You can do this by assuming responsibility for your life, and assuming responsibility for your self-assurance. By involving yourself in physical activities that will improve your fitness, and changing the way you view yourself, you can easily build your self-confidence without external assistance.

There are basic mediations planned for helping you increase your confidence:

Challenge Bad Thoughts about Yourself

To challenge bad thoughts about yourself, you need to come up with positive thoughts about yourself. This can be done by taking note of at least three things that you are good at. Try and remind yourself of and focus on what you are particularly good at when you are feeling low as they could help you feel better about yourself in those moments.

Whenever you have a negative thought, stop, and assess whether it is accurate. Search for evidence. Try to imagine what reaction you would have if a friend spoke about themselves in that manner. You would give them a more positive reply. Therefore, use the same method to challenge the negative thoughts that you get. Think of a more positive thought to replace a negative one.

You need to find methods to get to know more about the way in which you think of yourself. For example, when you are out there jogging or exercising, and your brain speaks to you, saying that it is hard, so you consider going back home and resting—this is the perfect example of a situation in which you can start overcoming your negative thoughts and think in a more positive manner. Thinking more positively enables you to live more positively. It might help to think of a negative thought as some type of obstacle that you need to get rid of.

When we have a low level of self-confidence, we often fear failure so much that we do not even attempt to do something that could potentially result in failure. To overcome this fear, think about the occasions you were frightened of accomplishing something, yet you attempted it anyway and ended up succeeding. It could be the first occasion when you plunged into a swimming pool, the first time you asked somebody out on a date, or the time you played an instrument before an audience at school.

This may appear to be unrelated but, think about these occurrences for a moment. We can defeat our negative thoughts. All the time, our brains overstate conceivable negative results and replay them again and again in our minds. A lot of our apprehensions are ridiculous. As Mark Twain stated, "I have gone through a large portion of my time on earth stressing over things that never occurred."

The normal individual has a huge number of considerations every day, and a considerable amount of these considerations is negative. We are continually conversing with ourselves in our minds, so it just generally a good idea to focus on the tone of our internal exchanges. We state and think things, for example, "I am a disappointment," "I can't be believed," "She can't be believed," "Life is uncalled for," "I am excessively short," "I can't do this," and so on. With consistent mindfulness, you can identify when you are having negative thoughts and work to replace them with positive ones.

Get to Know Yourself/Become Your Own Best Friend

A best friend is somebody you can trust with your most profound mysteries, somebody to depend on in times of emergency, and somebody to celebrate important life occasions with. Be that as it may, building up the courage to be your very own closest companion implies that you can depend on your judgment and be your very own source of solace when you need encouragement or support. Being your own best friend can likewise be an incredible method to work through sentiments of dejection, frailty, and confusion in your life. By developing a positive self, you can figure out how to confide in yourself consistently and refer to yourself in times of distress. Invest your energy in becoming acquainted with yourself. Consider what drives you, your preferences, and your strengths and shortcomings. We will, in general, search externally to make sense of our own preferences, thoughts, objectives, and interests, from social chit-chats around the water cooler at work to Facebook posts and Integra posts.

However, the more you understand yourself on a genuine level, the simpler it will be to accept yourself for who you truly are as opposed to who you think you are as a result of other individuals, patterns, and conditions throughout your life. Think about how you communicate with the individuals in your life, from your coworkers to your friends and family. Your attitude towards others reflects how you feel about yourself.

When a battalion is going to war, the commander must figure out long before the day of battle how to defeat the enemy. It is unwise to do so without getting to know the enemy well enough. In this regard, anytime you are attempting to beat the negativity in your mind, it is good to know that self-assurance is in yourself. Get to know yourself well by tuning into the things that are in your mind.

Write down the negative thoughts running through your head and consider why such thoughts would come to you. Afterward, take note of the things that benefit you, the things that make you progress in life positively, and the things that make you happy. On the other hand, take note of the things that restrict you and hinder you from developing positively, and note whether they are reasonable or could be done away with. By doing this, your self-assurance will grow in the end.

Fear is a feeling that every human being gets occasionally. It is a component that is necessary for keeping us safe and alive. However, when taken too far, it can start becoming demoralizing and debilitating. Fear causes a lack or loss in confidence in our abilities. When we acknowledge fear, we are able to manage it so as it won't affect our ability to make decisions as well as risk-taking that is vital in self-growth and helps us get out of our comfort zone.

Fear is a part of life; it is completely normal that we experience it occasionally throughout our lifetime. Individuals are not advised to be ashamed of being afraid as it is not a weakness. It is important to understand that fear exists anytime that we want to venture into things that are meaningful, but that should not stop us from engaging in these things. That is the meaning of courage. We need to be the drivers when fear comes along as a passenger.

Accept Yourself

First: Self-acknowledgment is vital to feeling certain about yourself and your abilities. At the point when individuals give you congratulations, just express profound gratitude as opposed to dismissing them or saying something negative.

Second: Nobody is perfect. Acknowledge your 'blemishes' or flaws and figure out how to cherish them. They are what makes you one of a kind—work it! Think about other individuals, too. They have flaws. They are always battling with their character; their life stays a steady process of acclimating to everyone's criticism. They try and please everyone and never end up satisfied with themselves. As people, we will, in general, get judgmental when we like the great pieces of our self and disdain the other pessimistic pieces of our mind. Refusal of the presence of our duality prompts concealment of the negative parts or not all the appreciated pieces of our being; we over and again would prefer not to feel and recognize its essence. In any case, they keep on existing within us—turning a blind eye doesn't change the truth.

This inability to acknowledge yourself as a good person, someone who is capable of anything they put their mind to, results in uneasiness and negativity. Naturally, accepting yourself for who you are and what you have, and can accomplish is the start of a bigger adventure; it opens you up to also acknowledging others for who they truly are and what they have and can accomplish. It enables you to identify with others wholeheartedly.

By this point, you should be able to recognize that you don't have to change who you are to accept who you are, even if you are not where you want to be in life. You should also be able to acknowledge the fact that every individual you interact with should also be accepted for who they are without anyone trying to change them. Once you have truly accepted yourself for who you are, you can use your newfound integrity to determine what jobs or careers to attain. Both now and in the future. You may have more to work on within yourself and in your life, but this will only enable you to take advantage of your known and obscure qualities. You will have the option to feel another surge of motivation and a strong desire to take on greater difficulties throughout everyday life.

Chapter 5: Who You Are for Your Family

The family is the first milieu to surround the child. It has effects on us practically from birth. We learn that the most important things in life are within our family, and that the basics of our self-esteem stem from the family. Our parents are the most important persons of our lives for several years, and they teach us many things; among them—the way we should see ourselves.

Spoken and unspoken parental evaluations of their children are greatly influencing the development of a child's self-esteem. Too many negative experiences and disappointments in the child's early years can lead to a disturbed sense of self. Parents' reactions and the quality of their care are the building blocks of the personality of children. These evaluations are especially important in early childhood when the independent personality of children is forming. It is similarly especially important in the sensible period of adolescence when teens are trying to find out who they are and where their place is in the world.

Parents sometimes use global words to describe a child as a complete being. He is "bad," because he is not able to play with other children at the playground and destroys what others have built. He is "dumb," because he is unable to learn two lines for the kindergarten festivity.

The truth is: no child is born as "bad" or "dumb," but these negative evaluations lead to negative feelings within the child and become parts of the forming identity of the child. Parents unconsciously or consciously plant negative seeds in their children. You can be sure that negative self-evaluations of six-year-old usually come from the spoken words of significant adults. "I cannot sing," "I cannot draw," "I am bad," "I am clumsy." Be careful what you say, parents, as your child usually believes everything you say to be factual and truthful. If they believe what you say, then they will reinforce it with time to be true.

On the other hand, parents can build a positive self-concept in their children as well. Acknowledging your child's skills and abilities is extremely important. Positive reinforcement and feedback for adequate performances and age-appropriate developmental tasks are great influences, which will shape self-image and self-evaluation in a positive way.

The parent's most important part in the development of self-esteem is probably their ability to serve as role models. The parent's attitude about themselves is often critical in the feedback given to their children. For example, when a parent is constantly unhappy about his or her body or physical appearance, the child will most likely display the same attitude as a teenager. It is important to learn to change things about us that we do not like and accept what cannot be changed.

Parental reactions to mistakes and failures of the child have a great influence. This is also mirroring the reaction to the parents' own shortcomings. A little humor makes small errors easier to tolerate.

Teenagers are especially likely to develop a negative voice within—"an inner critic." In many cases, this is based on the critical parent who they hear. Teens that feel that their parents have the qualities they admire, will develop a healthier self-esteem than those who do not feel like their parents have such assets.

The easiest way to build positive self-regard in our children is through the use of compliments and rewards. It is hard to tell how much positive reinforcement is needed, as much of it depends on the personality of the child. It is vital that compliments are meaningful and not just empty phrases.

Positive reinforcement should focus on the concrete, and if possible, avoid a general compliment, e.g. do not say: "You are clever or nice." Instead of saying that, try to use phrases that are connected to the actual situation: "You put away the toys neatly," or "You did a great job with your homework."

Failures that your children experience are easier to accept if you try to make your child a multifaceted personality. It would be great to help teach your child to be more tolerant of frustration. Praises should outweigh criticizing comments or critical observations. As a parent, it is important that you love your child with his or her mistakes and goof-ups, as well as when he/she is performing wonderfully.

Chapter 6: Overcoming Negative Thinking

Communication is a major part of our lives. From the time we are infants, our mind begins picking up language cues. Babies begin learning from the sounds of words and correlating facial expressions and context clues. It is like a puzzle, understanding what each word means. Communication is not only critical at these early stages of life—it continues to affect the relationships that people have with themselves and the people around them well into their adult lives.

How Your Script Shapes Your Life

The 'script' of your life describes all the conversations and words that you experience throughout the day. It is the interactions you have with others, as well as the words that you share with yourself. Think about the little voice in your head that you can hear when you are running late for work or when you are preparing for an interview or presentation. Is that voice talking you up? Is it telling you that you can handle what the day has in store and helping you prioritize, or is it causing you to feel overwhelmed or anxious? Does that voice make you feel confident before going into an interview or giving a presentation, or does it leave you imagining scenarios about what might go wrong?

One of the major things that set confident, successful people apart from those who feel 'stuck' in life is the way that they talk to themselves. People who portray confidence feel it from deep within. Instead of stressing over the many responsibilities they have that day, they feel confident that they can manage. They look at the day for the potential of opportunities and moving toward achievement—whether they are making strides with a new client or just catching up on housework. They are confident in meeting their goals and accomplishing what they set out to do.

For a comparison, let's consider how someone might experience their day after a rough morning. Think about the frustration you would feel if you woke up late for work, stubbed your toe on the door, and then dropped your yogurt on the floor—and that was only before work. This is a frustrating scenario that would upset anyone—but there are two ways to follow up a rough morning. For someone who struggles with self-confidence and self-esteem, this could be the beginning of an awful day. While they are in their car, hurrying to get to work, they might find themselves thinking, "I'm so stupid. Only lazy people show up late for work. Therefore, my boss won't give me a promotion. I'm a failure." A confident person might feel a little defeated after their morning, but they will ultimately shake it off. Their script in the car on their way to work might include things like "It is okay, the rest of the day will be better. I know I can turn today around. I'm ready to focus. People are late sometimes—I just made a mistake."

The person who has a negative script in the example is the person who is going to struggle turning their day around. By allowing their negative thoughts to govern their thinking, they are expecting a bad day. They might jump to conclusions or label something as bad, simply because that is how their mind is programmed to think about the day. By contrast, someone who talks to themselves with self-love and instills confidence in themselves is going to turn their day around. They'll arrive at work focused and ready to do their job, even though they are running late.

What Are Automatic Negative Thoughts?

Most people are familiar with the little voice in their heads that they hear throughout the day. It is the voice that tells them 'You've got this!' or 'Something will go wrong' before a presentation. The little voice exists in the conscious mind. This is the part of your mind that you have the most control over. It is the area where you rationalize and think things through. Often, however, the conscious mind 'hears' quick thoughts that come from nowhere. These are automatic negative thoughts (ANTs).

These thoughts that come from nowhere actually stem from the subconscious mind. The subconscious mind is like the catalog of the brain. For some people, it may be the root of problems like irrational fears, poor self-esteem, or anxiety. When you have an experience, the subconscious mind stores information about what happened, the emotions that you experienced with it, and the resulting actions. For example, someone who is bitten by a dog may not like dogs as an adult, even if they don't remember the incident. Some people may not like a specific type of dog breed, without really knowing why.

The reason people do not realize this is happening is that it takes less than a second for information to be passed through the brain. Inside the brain, there are close to a billion neurons. When you have a thought or respond to stimuli, the connection between certain neurons lights up. Think of this as a path in the woods. There are certain neurons that light up and send signals when a person is exposed to a dog if they are afraid of them. The first time this thought happens, it leaves behind a small trace. It is like flattened grass on a path. As this path is walked over again, it continues to wear down until the grass cannot grow there. Each time you have the same thought, it leaves a deeper imprint on your mind. This worn-down path can be traveled quickly. It has become a habit.

Many people experience automatic negative thinking at some point in their life.

Here are some of its characteristics:

- **Automatic** — the thought enters your mind without being consciously processed. It seems to come from nowhere.

- **Rapid** — these are fleeting thoughts that disappear in a fraction of a second.

- **Habitual** — It is not uncommon for ANTs to be considered normal by people who struggle with them. They are habitual for the brain, so they do not always demand attention. You may not even notice them.

- **Distorted** — distorted thinking describes thinking that has been twisted or altered in perspective. You'll learn more about this.

- **Situation-specific** — People do not realize there are patterns in their thoughts until they start looking for them. ANTs commonly occur in specific situations (like when you make a mistake or are running late).

- **Repetitive** — ANTs have themes related to the underlying issue. They might stem from a fear or a bad experience.

- **Condensed** — ANTs do not always make sense to other people. They may be symbolic or use some type of cognitive shorthand.

Common Automatic Negative Thoughts

While automatic negative thinking is always unique to the person with the thoughts, there are many patterns of thought. Look over this list and save it for later—it will help you identify your negative thinking.

- **Filtering** — filtering describes removing all the positive aspects of a situation and magnifying the negative details. By making the situation darker and more unpleasant, they distort it. People often do not realize they are doing this. They might have a minor disagreement with a coworker and a great lunch with their friend. Rather than focusing on the positives of the lunch, they let their day become dark and clouded by focusing on the disagreement.

- **jumping to Conclusions** — this distortion describes the action of assuming something with little evidence. They may assume that their spouse has been in a car wreck or is cheating if they are twenty minutes late coming home from work and cannot contact them. Jumping to conclusions can also be a sort of fortune-telling, where a person assumes someone feels a specific way toward them. For example, they may tell their boss 'hello' and he may not respond. Rather than thinking, he did not hear them; the person would assume their boss is mad at them.

- **Overgeneralization** — this type of thinking occurs when a single piece of evidence is used to 'prove' something. When something bad happens once, it is assumed it will continue to happen. For example, a college student who does poorly on a math exam might generalize they are bad at college math and drop out.

- **Black-and-White (Polarized) Thinking** — polarized thinking is also considered 'all-or-nothing' thinking. It is the inability to see the 'gray' area of things. Instead, the world is seen in black and white. This limits the complexity of situations, but it also causes a lot of negative thought.

- **Martyring (Heaven's Reward Fallacy)** — the idea behind being a martyr is generally religious. It is the idea that because a person goes through suffering, they are owed a greater reward later in life. This generally allows people to accept negatives on their lives but stops them from trying to achieve better because they believe it is meant to be.

- **Fallacy of Change** — this is the distorted impression that others will change with pressure. This is most common in relationships, where one of the partners believes they can make the other a better person. These relationships often end in disaster, as it is impossible to make someone change unless they want to do it themselves. Internal motivators are needed for change—not external ones.

- **Fallacy of Fairness** — People who claim things are 'not fair' believe they are entitled to better things in life. They may resent others who are more successful than they are or when they do not get this way.

- **Control Fallacies** — the control fallacy is distorted thinking that happens when a person uses two different beliefs to make something out of their control. For example, they may say it was not their fault they missed a deadline because they were driving back from their weekend vacation. (Even though they should have left earlier if they knew they had a deadline to work with). This is an external control fallacy. There are also internal control fallacies, where someone assumes more responsibility than they have. A friend may be in a car accident on the way to visit them and they will blame themselves for making plans, even though car accidents are unpredictable and can happen to everyone. They also may blame themselves when someone isn't happy.

- **Mr. Right** — someone who is always right is constantly putting others on trial to prove they are correct. They are determined to win arguments at any length. These types of people often struggle in relationships since they fail to take the emotions and feelings of others into consideration when they are proving their point.

- **Global labeling** — global labeling is the mislabeling of yourself or someone else from 1-2 pieces of evidence. Someone who struggles with this cognitive thought might experience a new coworker arguing with someone else and assume he is a jerk. They might get turned down by someone at the bar and assume they are unattractive, rather than considering the other person was in a relationship or uninterested. Usually, global labeling involves using emotionally loaded, vivid language.

Chapter 7: Assert Self-Love and Appreciation

Sound vanity is the absolute preliminary step to undertaking fact and identifying the way to be decisive. Without a truthful and solid diploma of self-worth, one can't be clear about what one has the right to have nor will she or he have the choice to approach others for what is needed or required. People without shallowness always will well know much less in mild of the reality that they do not understand they need to have extra. This text will help you with assessing your gift diploma of vanity and, within the event which you are inadequate close to, show you a way to construct it. It additionally will assist you with choosing in case your goals are excessively excessive and whether you observed your advantage greater without triumphing or work for it.

Evaluating and enhancing your cutting-edge level of self-worth

It is often difficult for us to have information into our very own characters, self-esteem, or even over the pinnacle pretention. Often, we can get exceptional input approximately these traits, or deficiency in that branch, from amazing loved ones. At the off threat that you have those, solicit their suppositions from your solid and feeble attributes and whether you must improve or mitigate your self-worth. At the off danger which you assume, your shallowness is low an instantaneous result of your circle of relatives, or your family is a poor judge of excellent passionate health, at that point you must abstain from drawing near family for his or her supposition. Making use of self-exams or the help of a decent expert may serve your wishes higher.

Take the vanity look below to find out your degree. Inside the event that your score is over 55 percentage and underneath 90 percent, you must discover a manner to improve your shallowness with the aid of tending to the troubles prompting your low self-confidence. You moreover can join each day in sporting events that enhance certainty. Peculiarly, do not be disturbed inside the event that your rating is below 90 percent; the maximum of people scores on this range.

Inside the occasion that your rating is under fifty-five percentage, you must address these issues speedily and start chipping away at them. More help from a guide is relatively prescribed.

Want to find out additional? Take an internet path in Assertiveness training.

To take an exhaustive vanity check incorporated by using Psychology today, scrutinize the accompanying connection.

Brain studies nowadays moreover offer a few top-notch self-assessments that will assist you with improving determine yourself in exceptional zones.

The differences between Low vanity, healthy self-esteem, and fake Ego individuals with sound shallowness do the accompanying:

- Like what their identity is.

- Are not reluctant to express their emotions or musings.

- Recognize they need to take a stab at something to accomplish greatness at it.

- Respect and fee the rights and tests of others.

- Do not must position others down to like themselves.

- Are geared up to well-known their imperfections and people of others.

- Are ready to gain from and well-known assist from others.

- Preference improvement, trade, and self-improvement.

- Set restrains in transit different individuals are approved to treat them.

- Are prepared to admit to committing a blunder.

- Have great limits and call for looking after them.

- Realize their restrictions.

- Respect their traits and shortcomings.

- Do no longer permit others to settle on poor selections for them.

People with low vanity show off these examples:

- Dislike themselves.

- Are particularly compromised through others.

- Are reluctant to express their sentiments.

- Need to discover shortcoming in others to find out worth in themselves.

- Engage in self-ruinous behavior.

- Surround themselves with self-ruinous people.

- Allow others to persistently deal with them seriously.

- Exaggerate their shortcomings.

- Do now not sense deserving of accomplishment.

- Sense vain or maladroit.

- Have problem tolerating and accepting commendations.

- Suppose everything is their flaw.

People with bogus internal self or gaudiness:

- Think they are superior to a terrific many humans.

- Have an elitist disposition.

- Have a sense of privilege and figure they do not want to buckle down for development.

- Disparage others' earned success, except if they can anticipate a reward for it.

- Cowl up their missteps or reprimand others for them.

- Assume their evaluation is the primary proper or possible one.

- Regularly specific checks that are not well-regarded into or dependent on trustworthy information.

- Have a twofold widespread for the way they live and how others live.

- Have hassle tolerating duty or fault for botches.

- Ingratiate themselves to those who will propel their social standing.

- Do now not discover an incentive in individuals except if they have riches or high social standing.

Daily Practices that growth Self-regard and healthful self-worth:

- Discover something to like approximately yourself.

- Locate something to like approximately any other person and let that character consider it.

- Exercise for on any occasion 20 minutes.

- Research something new.

- Spend time or chat with anyone you want who appreciates your conversation.

- Take time to prep yourself earlier than going out.

- Preserve your own home or apartment smoothly.

- Deliver actual commendations and acknowledge them nimbly.

- Do your best at something work you do; in the occasion which you are an understudy, supply a valiant attempt in college.

- Smile at yourself within the mirror and at others.

- Assist anyone who is out of luck or deliver to philanthropy; little alerts look at.

- Get a respectable night time's relaxation as regularly as may be predicted beneath the occasions.

- Recognize the quality endeavors of others.

- Congratulate yourself on any interest all round done.

- Cease.

Strong self-esteem and certainty are critical to being confident. Within the event which you have fundamentally low self-appreciate, you need to make enhancing your self-image your short commercial enterprise. Make use of the books recorded under simply as stable cherished ones to help you. At the off chance that vital, look for a proficient help from a respectable guide and explicitly permit him to realize or her that your objective is improving your self-esteem. At the off hazard which you fall into a mid-pass, as a super many human do, you must make investments some energy attempting to enhance how you experience approximately yourself as a person. Inside the event that you are a sense of right and wrong driven individual, your wishes are like people with low shallowness. It is far also as hard to get balance and earned self-worth at the off risk which you revel in the ill consequences of vainglory as although your vicinity no an incentive on yourself by any stretch of the imagination.

Your private level of Assertiveness Presentation

Each wish to select how agreeable the person is in speaking confidence. This stage depends on a super extent on the character's person kind. Diverse characters have numerous strategies for self-articulation that works for them. This region will acquaint you with the most famous man or woman sorts. Land up in these portrayals and use them to locate your very personal traits and shortcomings. While you recognize your special characteristics better, parent out a way to well known, be o.k. with, and utilize your very own satisfactory to nation your needs and desires to other humans.

Going with your Strengths

Considering you have got perused the man or woman sorts as well as have stepped via the exam, you need to have a superior concept of what your characteristics and shortcomings are. Since the character kinds are so expansive, you should now make this a stride further. On the following web page is a schedule. Utilize this rundown to record 10 of your very own qualities. A component of those will be super communicator, taken care of out, valid, powerful, inventive, remarkable cook dinner, a laugh, and so on.

At the factor when you have your rundown collectively, you likewise must put it to use to greater with no trouble renowned what you are high-quality at, what you need to accomplish professionally, what type of connections will work pleasant for you, and what type of existence will match your high-quality traits. You moreover will higher comprehend what you carry to the desk in the entirety of your connections, as it were, what you bring to the desk. Through understanding your traits, you realize what you need to apply to set up what you need, and need from individuals who have diverse characteristics. Information your features and enhancing them will boost your shallowness and finally, your actuality and potential to get up for yourself. You have got something to offer the sector, and it is essential to concentrate on building up your characteristics and improving your shortcomings to perform the maximum multiplied stage of self-truth.

Chapter 8: Creating Affirmations

The tone you adopt in the morning can dictate how the rest of the day might proceed. Why not set a positive tone for yourself? In fact, have you ever had an experience where you woke up in a state of panic, wondering if you forgot to complete an important task or if you are late for something, only to realize that nothing has happened and it was just your nerves? Or have you woken up once in such a state of stress that you could not even finish the coffee you made for yourself? All these situations have occurred because when you start your day poorly, the emotions trickle over to the next day. Eventually, you are living in a constant state of stress and negativity. Affirmations are simple phrases that help you focus on positive emotions. Every time you wake up, start the day with phrases like:

- Today, I shall face my day with courage and positivity.

- Today might be challenging, but so is any day of the week. I shall not let these challenges change my perspective of the world and create negativity.

- I am an incredible person and despite today's events, I will not look down on myself.

- Today is going to be a good day.

- I'm going to be awesome and nothing is going to convince me otherwise!

- You can always create your own positive affirmations depending on the situation.

Think About the Good Things, No Matter How Small They Are

Don't wait for a big moment to occur in your life. Look at every small event as another positive contribution. Here is the reality of life: no matter how much you want to avoid obstacles, you are going to encounter them every day. Each obstacle is something that has the potential to add to a whole pile of negative things. Eventually, you will feel that your life has too much negativity in it. What you are experiencing is small things that have accumulated to become something intimidating.

The same rule applies to the positive things in your life as well. Keep collecting them, no matter how little they seem. Eventually, the number of positive things will add up to become a dominating presence in your life.

Crank Up Your Humor

Don't let the dark situations get you down. Teach yourself to see the humor in things. Remind yourself that the situation you are in is going to get better eventually. After all, life goes on. Regardless of what happens to them, life is a continuous ticking clock. So, make a joke out of the things that have happened to you and move on.

Failures Are Lessons

Success finds those people who are not brooding over their failures but are finding ways to move past them. But the only way that can happen is if they choose to learn from their failures.

You too should approach your failures with tact and wisdom. Let your failures teach you a lesson; do not let them define your life. Bill Gates is defined by the success of Microsoft because he let that be the focus of his attention. If he had let his failures define him, then he would be in a different position rather than on the Forbes list of billionaires.

Watch Out for Negative Self-Talk

It's not unusual for people to berate themselves when they commit an error. How many times have you thought "I shouldn't have done it? I was going to fail anyway" when you tried something and didn't succeed at it? Or you might have thought one of these critical thoughts:

- Why do I even bother with such things anyway?

- What am I doing? I should have just stuck to what I know.

- If only I hadn't tried something new, this wouldn't have happened.

- Every time you create a negative statement about yourself, you are forcing your brain to think in a particular manner. And we don't need to go into the details of how your subconscious is going to latch on to those negative thoughts and run with them.

So, what should you do if you are faced with negative self-evaluations? You turn them into positive ones.

Let's say that you tried to do something, and it failed. Rather than thinking:

- I shouldn't have tried. This is what happens when you don't stick to what you do.

Think of it this way:

- So that's what happens if I do it this way! Interesting! I'll remember this and make sure I don't do it this way in the future. Or even if I do, I will plan better. Let's look at my other options.

Notice the difference? In the second response, you acknowledge that a mistake has been made. But you see it in a positive light. You allow it to teach you rather than defeating you. Make sure that you are not denying the fact that you have made a mistake. Denial has its consequences.

What is so bad about denial, you ask?

A lot.

One of the things that denial prevents you from doing is seeking help. We are not all perfect. Sometimes, we need help in our endeavors. That does not mean that we are weak or unskilled. It just means that we might need an extra pair of hands (or more) to help us with our project.

Denial also prevents us from acknowledging problems. If you feel that there are no problems, even when there are, then you won't learn to grow or deal with them. Eventually, those problems worsen and affect your life immensely later.

There are two things you can do with a problem. You can choose to face it and learn to handle it. Or you can choose to ignore it and watch it dismantle things in your life.

Among the two options, the ideal choice is obvious.

Focus on the Present

People often misunderstand this advice. They think that by being focused on the present, they must be aware of every ticking minute that passes by.

That's not true at all. The idea of being in the present—or practicing mindfulness as people like to say—is that you don't let your mind wander toward things of the past or events of the future. The reason for this is that the things of the past have already occurred and there is nothing you can do to change that. But, what about the things that are yet to happen? Use the steps below:

- **Step 1:** Can you deal with the situation? If yes, move on to Step 2, else move on to Step 5.

- **Step 2:** Have you already thought of ways to deal with the situation? If yes, move on to Step 5, else move on to Step 3

- **Step 3:** Can you come up with recommendations, ideas, or solutions to deal with the situation? If you yes, move on to step 4, else go to Step 5.

- **Step 4:** Do you have a plan of action? If yes, then move to Step 5, else create a plan of action and move to Step 5.

- **Step 5:** Continue with your day and bring your mind back to the present.

When you allow the past or present to occupy too much of your time in the present, then you might not perform well or achieve much in the present.

Have a Positive Circle of Friends?

Let me meet your friends and I can tell you what your future looks like. You might have heard that phrase repeated often. And for good reason. Since it does bear some truth.

When you surround yourself with friends who are positive influences in your life, you in turn improve your positivity.

Take this study conducted by Harvard psychologists as an example (Fowler & Christakis, 2008). The study was conducted over a period of 20 years and the results showed that happiness is greatly influenced by your social circles. In other words, you might very well be the company you keep.

When you surround yourself with positive people, their positivity seeps into your life. You become a sponge, absorbing their attitudes, and eventually adding certain quirks to your own personality.

Have friends who support you and accept you for who you are.

Hence, surround yourself with people who help you increase the positivity in your life.

Additionally, you can also find people who can act as your mentors. It could be your parents, siblings, friends, or even grandparents. Being in the company of positive people will allow you to learn from their attitudes. They might even be able to share some of their worldly wisdom with you.

Chapter 09: Calm Your Body

"Our bodies change our minds, and our minds can change our behavior, and our behavior can change our outcomes."

—Amy Cuddy

Andre was the communications director for a large company, but he lost his job in a corporate reorganization. After many years of feeling amazingly comfortable and confident in his position, he was now relegated to scouring online job boards, submitting applications, and hoping his résumé would interest a hiring manager.

Andre's background and résumé attracted considerable interest, and he was invited to several interviews. But each time, something seemed to go wrong. A couple of times Andre stumbled while answering a question. On other occasions, he had the gut feeling the employer was looking for someone younger.

Andre began to doubt himself. There must be something wrong with him to get rejected over and over for jobs for which he was highly qualified. When he asked his friends for help, they didn't seem to think the problem was his answers. Instead, it was how he was presenting himself. One friend suggested he shave his beard so he might look more youthful. Another said he needed to be more outgoing and friendly. His wife pointed out that when he was nervous, he came across as flat and distant. Each piece of well-meaning advice made Andre question more and more how he came across in the interviews. He realized knowing his stuff wasn't going to be enough to land a job. To be perceived as confident, he was going to have to fine-tune the messages he was sending with his body language, vocal inflections, and even his grooming.

In this chapter, you'll see that to build confidence, you have to ready your body as well as your mind. I'll teach you proven ways to calm your body so you can perform at your peak, even during stressful situations such as a job interview. You'll learn powerful mindfulness, gratitude, and relaxation techniques, in addition to gaining tips for general physical self-care. And finally, I'll lead you through some fascinating ways you can use your body posture to soothe your anxiety and express more confidence.

Revisit Your Goals

Do you relate to Andre's story? Think of a time when your body language may have been giving off a less-than-confident vibe or you felt so nervous that you couldn't perform up to your potential. On the lines below, describe what happened and how it felt.

Mindfulness

I touched on mindfulness and offered you a brief taste of a mindful breathing exercise. Recall that mindfulness is intentionally paying attention to the present moment with an attitude of openness, nonjudgmental, and curiosity. It's a way of inclining the mind in a useful direction. You've heard the phrase, "You are what you eat." The same can be said for our minds: We are what we pay attention to. By directing your attention in a certain way, mindfulness will help you develop greater calm at your core, making it more likely you'll tackle even your toughest challenges. A strong mindfulness muscle, built through regular practice, is an important tool to have in your self-confidence tool kit.

Before we move on, I want to dispel a few myths about mindfulness that may get in the way of your approaching this section with an open mind.

Mindfulness Myths

•You do not have to believe anything to practice mindfulness. Although many religions have contemplative practices (e.g., meditation, centering prayers), the versions you'll learn here are secular.

•Mindfulness is not something exotic, mysterious, or reserved for a special few. You don't have to sit cross-legged, and you don't have to burn incense (but you can if you want to).

•Mindfulness may or may not involve formal meditation. Some people develop a regular meditation practice once they get a taste of mindfulness, but this is not necessary.

•Mindfulness is not a cure-all. As mindfulness has entered the mainstream culture, the implication has been that it's so powerful it can cure everything from depression to chronic pain. While it can help with many conditions, it's generally not a stand-alone treatment. If you suffer from clinical depression or an anxiety disorder, or have a history of trauma, please work with a mental health professional.

Have you tried mindfulness before?

- Yes
- No

What has been your experience?

- Positive
- Negative
- Neutral

Check any of the mindfulness myths that you've ever believed:

- Mindfulness involves religion.
- Mindfulness is mysterious.
- You must meditate to practice mindfulness.
- Mindfulness will cure all your problems.

Mindfulness Basics

The steps of most mindfulness practices share common instructions:

Bring your attention to the present moment. To facilitate this, you'll select an object of attention. It can be the breath, but it could be the sounds around you, sensations in a part of your body (for example, the hands), or the experience of the whole body.

Observe what's happening at that moment. If you're focusing on the breath, notice where you feel the breath most strongly—at the nostrils, perhaps the chest, or maybe the abdomen. If you'd like, you can silently say; "In," on the inhale and, "Out," on the exhale. This is a soft mental note to help you stay focused. If you're focusing on your hands, you can ask; "Do they feel warm? Are they tingling?" By focusing on your present moment experience, you'll be able to disengage more easily from the past, which you can't change, and the future, which is uncertain.

Notice when your attention has strayed. It may be a few seconds or a few minutes into your practice, but you'll wake up and realize that you've been lost in a long story (what your boss said to you yesterday) or a short complaint (your leg is falling asleep). No problem! It doesn't mean you've done anything wrong. Meditation expert Sharon Salzburg calls this "the magic moment," and believes it to be a crucial aspect of the practice. The point when you notice your mind has wandered is the moment when you have a chance to do it differently. Instead of scolding yourself by thinking, "I am so bad at this," be gentle with yourself and simply start again, refocusing on your object of attention.

That's it. The three basic instructions are simple, although you'll find they're not always easy. Practice helps a lot, and so do the following tips.

Mindfulness Tips

If you're a beginner, here are some practical ways to work mindfulness practices into your daily life. Set a goal to spend just a few minutes being mindful each day. If you want to devote more time to your practice, you can refer to the Resources for books, apps, and podcasts that can help.

Find your style. If you sit at your desk all day, practicing mindfulness on a chair or cushion at home may not be what you need. A walking mindfulness practice may suit you better.

Be flexible. Some people suffer from chronic pain or other health conditions, and prolonged sitting is difficult. Magazine covers show young bodies sitting in the lotus position, but you can practice while sitting, lying down, walking, or standing. Listen to your body, and practice in whatever pose works for you.

Keep your expectations realistic. Remember that mindfulness isn't going to solve all your problems and make your life constantly peaceful.

One thing I hope you'll discover: Although you may not find anyone mindfulness session particularly impressive, over time, you'll notice the effects in your life. For example, you'll instinctively pause before you hit Send on that critical email, or you'll more quickly refocus when you're being a jerk to yourself. Mindfulness will pave the way to a more positive and confident you.

One-Minute Mindfulness

Here are a few exercises you can try that will take no longer than a minute:

1. Notice that you're safe right now. Are you breathing? Check. Jon Kabat-Zinn reminds us, "If you're breathing, there's more right with you than wrong with you."

2. Take a deep breath, imagining you're breathing in white light as you inhale and breathing out dark clouds as you exhale. Repeat.

3. Pet your cat or dog and immerse yourself in the sensations of your hand touching its fur. Allow your pet's unconditional loving gaze to seep deep inside you.

4. Do this "5-4-3-2-1" exercise that engages all your senses: Take note of five things you can see, four things you can hear, three things you can touch, two things you can smell, and one thing you can taste.

5. Pretend you must write a letter to a friend describing this moment with as much evocative detail as possible.

What do you notice around you? How would you set the scene?

6. Focus for a moment on each part of your body from toes to head, thinking to yourself with each breath, "Let my feet be at ease (...) Let my calves be at ease (...) Let my knees be at ease," and so forth.

7. Take a minute during a meal to set distractions aside and focus on the experience of eating. Taking slow bites, notice the aromas and flavors of the dish and the gratitude you feel for the meal.

8. Visualize a stream flowing past you. Each time a thought pops into your head, imagine the thought as a leaf on the stream, slowly passing by and out of view.

9. Think about your hands. What have your hands done for you today? Notice any worries or judgments about each hand. What sensations do you feel in your hands right now? Let your thoughts come and go.

10. Pick an object in your surroundings and pretend you've never seen it before. With openness and curiosity, notice its color, texture, shape, and shadow.

Relaxation

Stress can make you feel out of control, which undermines self-confidence. When you feel out of your depth or are facing a challenge that matters a lot to you, physical symptoms of anxiety are almost sure to follow. A racing heart and sweaty palms can draw your attention away from the moment, but with some practice, you can learn to soothe yourself through relaxation techniques.

By relaxing, you not only train the body to react differently to events going on around you; you also change the way you think about situations or tasks that used to fill you with dread.

Chapter 10:

5 Steps to Healthy Self-Esteem: Know Yourself, Care, Respect, Accept, Love Yourself

Know Yourself

Knowing yourself is the first step to building your self-esteem. When you have a solid grasp of who you are today, where you have come from, and what experiences have impacted your self-image, you can move forward toward improved self-esteem. Self-awareness allows you to identify where you lack self-esteem, understand exactly how low self-esteem negatively impacts your life, and make changes to improve self-esteem. This step involves getting in touch with who you really are, and the process can be transformative. From there, you can begin really taking ownership of your life and readily understand and change any negative aspects that may have contributed to low self-esteem.

Women with healthy self-esteem usually know themselves well. They acknowledge both their strengths and weaknesses, recognize the various factors that have played a role in their development, and generally feel in control of their lives. They take responsibility for personal courses of action, despite how others may act, and are able to separate external influences from their core sense of self. This encompasses characteristics like independent-mindedness, security, and not being overly sensitive. Conversely, women with low self-esteem have become disconnected from their own selves. They see themselves through a faulty lens and sometimes view themselves as simply an extension of other people. They often neglect to cultivate their own identity and tend to routinely sacrifice their own identities to care for others. By nature, women are nurturing caretakers and good attending to the needs of others; however, when a woman endures years of low self-esteem, she becomes susceptible to taking care of everyone but herself.

Women with low self-esteem may constantly try to please others while losing themselves in the process. Take, for example, a woman who hates sports but pretends to love football so, the new guy she's dating thinks she's cool and fun. She ends up doing things like this to please others and be accepted, to the point that she forgets who she really is and what she genuinely likes and dislikes. When you become so far removed from your own thoughts, ideas, and opinions, it becomes difficult to remember or recognize who you are. Identifying even considerably basic likes and dislikes can become a challenge.

Part of knowing yourself involves familiarizing yourself with who you truly are today. The following exercise allows you to spend some time thinking about your own identity, including what you like and what your hopes and dreams are. Watch out for any thoughts that might pop up regarding the expectations, demands, or desires of others, instead, answer the following questions based solely on your own gut and intuition. It may take some time to come up with answers, but that's okay. Take your time and answer any questions you can, and feel free to skip over ones that seem too difficult to complete at this stage.

Caring for Yourself

It is well established as the path to well-being, but it is less obviously recognized as a critical factor in developing and maintaining healthy self-esteem. Caring for every aspect of your identity is vital to developing a sense of self-worth.

By caring for yourself physically and emotionally, you send yourself and others the message that you are important and worthy. When you fail to care for yourself, you send powerful and damaging signals to yourself that you are unimportant and insignificant. Caring for yourself involves treating yourself well, making healthy choices, and prioritizing your own well-being. In this step, we will look at specific ways you can implement self-care tools that will contribute to developing healthier self-esteem.

Creating a Habit of Caring Self-Talk

As we explored in the last step, the way we think, and our internal voice dictates our feelings and moods, contributes to our level of self-esteem. Once you come to know yourself and can identify the negative patterns in your thinking, the next step is to begin challenging and reframing these thoughts into messages that are more caring and self-nurturing. By taking better care of yourself through the way you think and talk, you can improve self-esteem and live a more fulfilling life.

Changing unproductive patterns in thinking and behavior is the basis of cognitive-behavioral therapy, an effective, evidence-based method for treating issues like anxiety and depression, and improving overall mental health. Changing negative self-talk is a straightforward concept: replacing the habit of thinking negatively with a healthier practice of thinking in more rational and encouraging ways.

Respect Yourself

Knowing who you are and caring for yourself are the fundamental steps in developing the necessary understanding and self-compassion to reclaim feelings of self-worth. However, you can't truly develop and maintain healthy self-esteem until you can consistently respect yourself. While self-esteem involves how you think and feel, self-respect is about your actions. How you act and interact with others and the choices you make relate to your level of self-respect and ultimately play a role in your view of self-worth. Self-respect, along with a determination to begin making healthier choices, will help you make the most of the tools provided in the last steps.

Women who make destructive or self-deprecating decisions that demonstrate a lack of self-respect stay trapped in a cycle of low self-esteem. When you fail to make healthy changes, acting in self-denying ways, or make poor choices, this inevitably leads to negative self-talk that further depletes self-esteem. In this case, you must work twice as hard to block negative messages as you find a way to rationalize your actions, inactions, or self-destructive decisions. When you make bad decisions that harm yourself or others, you feel bad about who you are and feel out of control, making healthy self-esteem exceedingly difficult.

Accept Yourself

Once you have made strides in getting to know yourself and have committed to practicing better self-care and treating yourself with respect, the next step is to develop true acceptance of who you are. This is a real turning point in the path to self-esteem. Accepting yourself involves coming to terms with the reality of your humanity, accepting your limits, acknowledging your shortcomings, and recognizing that maintaining healthy self-esteem is a lifelong journey.

Gaining perspective and realistic standards are key to finding the self-acceptance necessary to build self-esteem. This step is where you really begin to recognize and accept yourself as imperfect yet whole. Until you truly accept yourself, you will remain vulnerable to the devastating effects of negative self-talk and distorted messages that block the path toward improved self-esteem.

Self-acceptance doesn't happen in a moment; rather, it is an evolution. It involves working through your feelings and dissecting your past experiences to come to appreciate who you are. It's about acknowledging the different traits, experiences, and encounters that make up your existence, and coming to terms with the fact that you are going to have weaknesses. Self-acceptance is about being okay with yourself no matter what has happened or where you are today. In this chapter, you'll learn how to ward off the demons that can sabotage self-esteem as you develop a more secure and forgiving view of yourself.

Love Yourself

Accepting yourself sets the stage for loving yourself, which is the final step in your journey to obtaining healthy self-esteem. When you are truly able to love yourself, you become capable of treating yourself with the compassion, flexibility, and affection that are so important to maintaining self-esteem throughout life. Loving yourself involves acknowledging and accepting that you deserve love and that others around you benefit from your love; not only your love for them but for yourself as well.

There's a reason that many of the buzzwords and steps in this journey involve the word self—self-esteem, self-worth, self-knowledge, self-care, self-respect, and self-acceptance. You cannot accomplish any of these things through external means. Building self-esteem and cultivating a life of confidence and inner strength requires you to turn inward, take small risks for positive change, and embrace vulnerability, all things that are most successfully accomplished when backed by love and support.

By accepting and loving yourself from within, you can maintain healthy, loving relationships built on mutual respect. Strong relationships require self-esteem, and they also help to support it. When we love ourselves and others, we can reap the important benefits of healthy self-esteem.

The idea of self-love may seem simplistic; however, it's often one of the most difficult steps to achieve for women with low self-esteem, who have likely suffered years of believing they are not lovable. Absolutely loving yourself can require hard work and a willingness to be vulnerable, but the rewards are immense. It may feel silly or foreign at first to think about loving yourself but accessing the ability to cultivate self-love has an enormous impact on the path that awaits you beyond this journey. In this chapter, you will learn how to love and protect yourself in ways that will foster healthy self-esteem.

Chapter 11: Believe in Yourself

Developing a Stronger Sense of Self Leads to Self-Confidence

Knowing and respecting your goals and values is an important part of self-confidence. Unfortunately, it's all too common for people to set aside their authentic self in order to please others.

Here are some ideas to help you develop a stronger sense of self:

Become Comfortable with Being Alone

If you want to do something, don't wait for others to join you. Go to a movie, or to an event you're interested in. Being by yourself may even be more enjoyable because you can focus all your attention on what you're doing.

Set and Keep Boundaries

Be clear on what you will and will not do. If you're afraid of disappointing others, you may find yourself doing a lot of things you don't want to do.

Go Your Own Way

Don't be afraid to do your own thing even if it goes against what everyone else is doing.

Don't Compare Yourself to Others

We're all on different paths and different stages in our lives. While it's tempting to compare, we to others, remember that what you see or think is going on, is probably not the reality.

List Past Successes and Use Them to Your Advantage

Taking stock of our wins is an excellent way to build our confidence. Write down your successes and the things which you're especially proud of. Keep your list in a journal where you can review it regularly, and especially when you've suffered a setback or are feeling discouraged.

Another good practice is to keep a daily list of small wins. These aren't the big victories like promotions, awards, and milestones. These accomplishments can be as simple as staying on track with your diet, not losing your temper in a frustrating situation, and starting a new class.

When you're climbing a mountain and see how far you still have to go, it can be easy to forget how far you've already come. Recording your accomplishments is an enormous confidence-booster because it's a reminder that of how much progress you've made.

Get Feedback from Others

Constructive criticism is a valuable tool if we know how to accept it. If you're working on a project, or learning a new skill knowing what you're doing right and where you need improvement will help you do a better job.

Be open-minded and don't be defensive when hearing from others. Remember you want to improve and that comes with time and effort.

Replace Negative Beliefs with Positive Ones

This is one of the most valuable skills you can master and will be invaluable in your confidence building journey so we're going to spend quite a bit of time on this topic.

Confronting negative thoughts can feel impossible. You start to make progress and your inner critic kicks in again and you lose your momentum. You may start to wonder if you'll always be paralyzed by negative thoughts. Don't worry, self-doubt is natural. But that doesn't mean that your inner critic will always be in control of your mind.

I just know I'm going to get fired!

I'm a terrible parent.

I'll be alone for the rest of my life.

We all have the occasional negative thought. But many people battle negative thinking constantly. They're bombarded with thoughts which all revolve around one thing: telling them how worthless they are.

There are ways to handle negative thinking in a healthy way. Learning how to handle negative thinking in a healthy way will allow you to act and build self-confidence.

Our minds have a constant stream of thoughts running through them. Some of them are neutral, others are even pleasant. And of course, we have some that are negative. These negative thoughts aren't the real problem—it's the power we give them. If you choose to believe your negative thoughts, they'll erode your self-confidence and even stop you from moving forward in your life.

Common Types of Negative Thoughts:

Assumptions

When you make assumptions, you're filling the unknown with undesirable outcomes. Several good things are also possible. But your negative thoughts don't allow you to see those possibilities.

The "Should"

When you start thinking about all the things you should have done, or you should be doing, you're comparing yourself unfavorably and deciding that you fall short. This attitude shakes your confidence and makes it harder for you to reach your goals.

Black-and-White / All or Nothing

Black-and-white thinkers (also known as all or nothing) believe that things are either all good or all-bad, there's never a happy medium. So, if you failed a test, you immediately think you're a failure. If you have a fight with your spouse, then the relationship is doomed.

But you can't place things into black and white categories and once you realize that you'll be a lot happier. You'll no longer be worried about what you must or should do. You understand that there are "what if's" and "maybes," and that the all or nothing perceptions are all in your mind.

Catastrophizing

Shifting from making assumptions to imagining an all-out worst-case scenario is called catastrophizing. A failure becomes insurmountable and it's easy to lose sight of reality.

Can you see any of your negative thoughts on this list? It's a good idea to start recording the negative thoughts that pop into your head. Eventually, you'll be able to recognize a pattern.

When you write a negative thought down, ask yourself if it's true or not. Then list the evidence that supports either conclusion.

How to Eliminate Negative Thinking

Now that you are aware of your negative thoughts, you can start to break free of them. Don't get frustrated if you find it difficult at first. Let's review a few techniques to help you work through these nagging thoughts.

Reframe Your Negative Thoughts

The next time you work on dismantling a negative thought, ask yourself a couple of questions. Is this thought helpful? Is it helping me move toward my goals or is holding me back?

If that doesn't work, try to reframe the thought in a more positive way. If you think that you're stupid because you never learned how to swim, tell yourself that you're proud of yourself for taking the steps to gain a skill you've always wanted to have.

You can also reframe your feelings. If you feel anxious, tell yourself that you feel this way because you're about to do something that is important to you. Instead of anxiety, reframe your feelings as excitement.

Remove Your Attachment to the Thought

Instead of saying: "I'm a loser," switch it to "I'm having the thought that I'm a loser." This is an important distinction even if it seems like a small thing because you gain the perspective that you are not your thoughts.

Visualize your negative thought as a balloon and imagine it floating away. Continue with each new, negative thought, and those all float away.

Another technique is to thank your mind. If you're worried that the plane you're on is going to crash, thank your mind for being concerned about your safety.

Avoid Generalizations

Watch out for absolute terms like: "always," "never," "all," "none." These words usually indicate black-and-white thinking. Make your self-talk as balanced and specific as possible.

If you're thinking: "I always screw things up," change the thought to: "Sometimes things don't go the way I planned. Sometimes they do, and sometimes they even go better than expected."

Calm Your Inner Critic

You can't get rid of your inner critic, but you can learn how to keep it calm and take away its power. Give it a name like Negative Nancy. Remember that it has good intentions; it's trying to save you from potential failure or embarrassment.

Identify Your Negative Core Beliefs

Your core beliefs are the principles that guide you through life. They can be positive or negative. When they're self-limiting, they trick your mind into seeing the world as more dangerous than it is.

There are several common core beliefs, see if any of these resonate with you:

- I don't belong.

- The world is dangerous.

- I'm a failure.

- I must be perfect.

- People can't be trusted.

- Life is full of heartbreak and despair.

- My needs aren't important.

Conclusion

By the end of this book, you should be feeling like you have gotten a good understanding of the fundamentals of self-esteem and the components in your life that you would need to change in order to boost it. Just to recap, you have learned that self-esteem is not the same as self-confidence and what the fundamental differences are. You learned the importance of each and why they work hand in hand to enable a person to have a healthy mental wellbeing. You also explored the different causes of low self-esteem and how it typically starts in a person's childhood. After that, you explored all the different benefits that come with increasing a person's self-esteem. This was extremely important as understanding these benefits will become the driving factor behind all the hard work that you are going to do to increase your own self-esteem. Then, you explored all the benefits that come with improving self-confidence, which in turn also helps you with self-esteem. After that, you explored an important chapter where you learned to identify what your level of self-esteem is. You learned that the self-esteem spectrum ranges from low self-esteem to high self-esteem with healthy self-esteem in the middle. You also learned those people with high self-esteem don't mean that they have healthy self-esteem and in fact, it is just a technique to cover up the fact that they have low self-esteem. You did various exercises throughout these 10 steps and this is likely the longest you've had to work through. You began to learn about other components of self-esteem like self-acceptance and self-awareness. These components play a big role in a person's ability to boost self-esteem as they all have a strong relationship with one another. Lastly, you were provided with a chapter that is just full of additional worksheets you can use to help gain more self-esteem. These are extremely important as it is easy to fall back into old habits if one does not continue to try in completing the practices for self-esteem.

Now that you have excellent knowledge of everything to do with self-esteem and how to increase it, what are the next steps? The short answer for you is consistency. You learned that self-esteem fluctuates depending on a person's circumstance. By continuing to remind yourself of how self-esteem works and continuing to do exercises even if you have healthy self-esteem will prevent it from fluctuating a lot when you are faced with an obstacle in life. We learned that it is silly to think that a person's journey through life would be smooth and obstacle-free. By continuing to practice exercises and completing worksheets to help build a more positive inner self, you are well-equipped to handle obstacles on your own when they do arise.

One of the last messages that I want to get across to you is how important consistency is moving forward from this book. You are the only person that can hold you accountable to continue completing exercises and practicing the self-care needed to have a healthy self-esteem. I provided you with a quick guide in self-care that has a list of components that you should be doing every day to maintain a healthy lifestyle. By feeling healthy, positive, and energized, a person is more likely to feel good about themselves which is a great self-esteem boost. However, being stuck in unhealthy habits like eating badly, avoiding social contact, or sleeping irregularly are all habits that decrease a person's self-esteem. Remember that even someone who has always had healthy self-esteem is still at risk of having low self-esteem depending on their life situation, their outlook on the world, and their ability to deal with problems. Nobody is 100% shielded from developing low self-esteem. The only thing you can do is to keep maintaining your self-esteem so there is a lower chance that an obstacle or situation in your life can bring you down.

The exercises throughout this book are designed to help anyone that is looking to grow or maintain their self-esteem. A common theme that I tried to emphasize throughout your journey is that simply doing these exercises once will not be helpful in the long run. For a person to see long term success, they are going to have to incorporate these exercises into their daily routine. For example: we went through an exercise where you wrote out in a chart a list of people that could use your help and what you were going to do to help them. Only doing that once during your assignment of the exercise will only provide short term benefits. However, if you incorporate helping someone every day or even every week, you are getting into the habit of doing well for your community and providing yourself with a sense of fulfillment. This holds true for all the other exercises that you are provided. When you get to the point where you have finished all the worksheets in this book, simply just start over from the beginning. Keep doing this until it becomes a habit and these exercises will simply become reinforcement for your self-esteem rather than a boost. In conclusion, I'd like to thank you for taking the initiative in changing your life. The easier option is to just go along with how things have always been and find coping mechanisms to deal with unfortunate things that happen. Instead, you took the harder route and decided to find ways to change yourself into someone that you can be happy with. This doesn't mean that you are trying to accomplish more goals or become more successful. This simply means that you are beginning to practice being happy with who you are and accepting everything about yourself regardless of good or bad. Remember, self-esteem isn't about accomplishing more things so you can feel good about yourself, it is about changing the way you see yourself and the ability to a perception that is more positive. In turn, you will gain more confidence about your ability which will motivate you to try new things and pursue new goals. When you start doing that, which is when you will start seeing success in your life. As much as a low self-esteem can be a vicious cycle, having a healthy self-esteem is a good cycle as accomplishing goals helps you build more self-esteem, and having more self-esteem helps you work harder to achieve goals. So again, I'd like to thank you for taking the time to change your life for the better. Remember, if you feel like you've fallen off track, simply just pick up this book again and start from the beginning.

CPSIA information can be obtained
at www.ICGtesting.com
Printed in the USA
BVHW070858150321
602550BV00010B/1128